TWIN FLAME

WHO ARE YOU?

JEEVITA GOWD

Made with ❤ on the Notion Press Platform
www.notionpress.com

I WANT TO DEDICATE THIS BOOK TO MYSELF .

FOR ENDURING ALL THE PAIN ALL ALONE .

Contents

Preface

THIS BOOK IS ALL ABOUT
THE LOVE BETWEEN THE
TWO PERSONS
WHO NEVER MEET.
WHEN THEY STARTED LOVING
EACH OTHER WITHOUT
KNOWING EACH OTHER

Acknowledgements

I WOULD LIKE TO SAY THANKS
MY LATE MOTHER .
AND THANKS FOR MYSELF FOR
NOT GIVING UP ON MYSELF WHEN
WHOLE WORLD LEFT MY HAND .
THIS BOOK IS PENNED AND EDITED
BY ME WITH MY OWN IMAGINATION.

Prologue

THIS BOOK IS ABOUT TWO PERSONS .
WHO NEVER MEET EACH OTHER
BUT FALLEN IN LOVE .
WITHOUT KNOWING ABOUT
THEIR EXISTENCE .
THEY BOTH BELIEVED THEY EXIST
SOMEWHERE IN THIS WORLD .
EVEN AFTER HAVING EVERYTHING
THE EMPTINESS BETWEEN THEM
COULDNOT BE ERASED WITH THE TIME.
A FEW LETTERS THEY WANTED TO
GIVE THEM BEFORE THEY LEAVE
THIS WORLD .
THEY WANT TO SEARCH THEIR
EXISTENCE IF THEY REALLY EXIST
OR ITS JUST A DREAM THEY ARE
LIVING FOR.
WOULD DIVINE TIMING LET THEM
MEET AND CONVEY THEIR MESSAGES ?
OR THEY LOOSE BEFORE THE FATE ?
A LONELY LETTER OF A GIRL TO
UNKNOWN SOMEONE .

Author Bio

MEET THE AUTHOR MISS JEEVITA GOWD
SHE IS AN AUTHOR BY PASSION AND MODEL.
SHE COMPLETED HER GRADUATION.
HER HONOURS –
SHE WAS THE CO –AUTHOR OF 5 BOOKS
AND AUTHOR OF THE BOOKS
1-THE WAY TO SUCCESS BY
ACCEPTING PAIN AND REALITY
2- LOVE STORY OF ALICE AND DANID.
3-CURSED ISLAND .
4-BOOK OF QUOTES
5-FADED DREAM OF PAST LIFE.
6-SUCCESS MINDSETS
AND IN WRITING FIELD SHE
ACHIEVED MOST PRESTIGIOUS AWARD
GLORY AWARD OF INDIA AS AN AUTHOR.
SHE IS FAMOUS HER QUOTES
SHE WAS FEATURED MANY MAGAZINES
LIKE TIMES OF SRINAGAR,
TIMES OF AMERICA
TIMES OF UP
TIMES OF BOMBAY
HER HONOURS AS A MODEL
MISS BHARAT OF CHATTISGARH WINNER
MISS REPUBLIC OF INDIA SECOND RUNNER
AND SHE ALSO WALKED IN
INTERNATIONAL RAMP.
CAN SHOW LOVE ON
-INSTAGRAM-AUTHORJEEVITA

Author Pick

AUTHOR PICK

CHAPTER ONE

WHO ARE YOU?

TWIN FLAME

MAY BE THERE ARE VAGUE OF DIFFERENT EMOTIONS A PERSON HAS BUT THEY ARE UNAWARE .
MAY BE IN LIFE WE CAN MEET THOUSANDS OF PEOPLE BUT EXCEPT A SINGLE PERSON EVERYTHING FEELS WORTHLESS.
MAY BE EVERY PERSON CHANGES WHEN THEY MEET A PERSON WHO CAN CHANGE THEIR WHOLE WORLD .
WE CANT FORCE ANYTHING TO TAKE PLACE BUT SOMETIMES WE CAN CONTROL OUR EMOTIONS .

MAY BE SOMETIMES OUR HEART FEELS SO DEPTH WITHOUT KNOWING THE REASON .

IT ACHES TO THE DEATH MAY BE IT
UNDERSTOOD THE DEPTH OF EMOTIONS
WHICH WE HUMANS CANT SEE IT .
WHEN RAIN COMES I SEE THE
DISAPPEARING MOON WITHOUT
KNOWING MY HEART FEELS SO
HEAVY TO SEARCH SOMETHING
WHICH I NEVER KNOWN .

IN LIFE I EXCEPT THINGS TO BE DEEPER .
I EXPECT PURE LOVE IN THE WORLD OF
HAVING TIMEPASS.
I WISH TO SEE AN INNOCENT EYES
WHICH MAKES ME FEEL THIS IS WHAT
IS HAVE BEEN WAITING FOR THE AGES .

MAY BE I AM SEARCHING FOR
SOMETHING IN THIS WORLD
WITHOUT KNOWING WHAT IT
WAS .
MAY BE SOMETHING WHICH CAN
ADD MEANING TO MY EXISTENCE.
THE LIFE IS FULL OF MYSTERY
SOMETIMES WHAT WE FEEL AND
WHAT WE SEE IT IS DIFFICULT TO
EXPLAIN BECAUSE SOME FEELINGS
DOESN'T HAVE THE NAME FOR IT.

THIS WORLD THERE WOULD BE A
PERSON WHO WOULD BE WAITING
IN THE RAYS OF DARKNESS .
MAY BE THAT PERSON WOULD
BE PURE MIRROR TO YOU AND
THAT WORTH WAITING FOR IT.

I BELIEVE IN SPIRTUAL POWERS
I FEEL THE THINGS DEEPER .
THERE ARE MANY UNKNOWN
PUZZLES OF MY LIFE HAS BEEN
ALWAYS REMAINED UNSAID .
MAY BE ONE DAY I CAN SEARCH
THE ANSWERS OF UNSOLVED
DREAMS.
I BELIEVE IN 3D WORLD YOUR
EVERY PHENOMENM WILL
REFLECT ANOTHER YOU IN
THE WORLD .
THE DEPTH OF SOME
QUESTIONS WILL ALWAYS
REMAIN HIDDEN.

MAY BE EVERY PERSON YOU MEET IN
THIS LIFE MAY NOT MEET WITH
CONCIDENCE EVERY PERSON HAS

CONNECTION WITH THE PAST LIFE.
THE TIME IT END THE RELATION
WITH THE PERSON ENDS.
SUNSETS MAKES ME BELIEVE
THERE IS SOMETHING BEAUTIFUL
IN THE RAYS OF DARKNESS .
I LOVE DARKNESS BECAUSE I SEE MY
TRUE SELF IN THIS AND I AM NOT
AFRAID OF PEOPLE TO SHOW MY
FLAWS BECAUSE BEING BROKEN
HAS ITS OWN BEAUTY .
I AM A TYPE OF PERSON WHO IS
INTROVERT DON'T LIKE TO GO
OUT ENJOY MY OWN COMPANY
PERFECT IN MANY ASPECTS BUILT
MYSELF IN THE DARKNESS .
CROSSED JOURNEY IN THE WAY
OF THRONES .
WILL I BE OK SOMEDAY?
IN THE WORLD WHICH NEVER
SUITS ME BUT I AM OK WITH
THIS PAIN AND SURELY I AM
WILLING TO WAIT UPTO THAT
MOMENT WHERE THIS BLEED IN
HEART WILL STOP AND SAY THIS
IS WHAT I AM SEARCHING FOR .
MAY BE I CANT BE OK BUT I CAN
BEAR THIS.
SOMETIMES I FEEL PITY ON
THIS HEART .
FOR FEELING DEPTH FOR EVERY
EMOTIONS AND TAKE THINGS
WHICH MAKES LIFE BURDEN .

TO THE PEOPLE WHO NEVER
MEANT TO BE IN THE LIFE.
THE MOONS MAKES ME KEEP
BURDEN ON MY HEART WAITING
FOR SOMETHING WHICH CAN
MAKE FEEL ALIVE .
SOMETIMES IT FEELS SO STRANGE
FOR NOT KNOWING WHAT THIS
HEART IS WAITING OF MY LONELY
SOUL .
I WISH TO HAVE SOMEBODY IN MY
LIFE WHOM I CAN CHEERISH MY
REST OF LIFE AND EXPRESS HOW
BEAUTIFUL THE WORLD IS WITH
THAT ONE PERSON WHO CAN MAKE
ME FEEL ALIVE .
EVEN THROUGH I AM DIFFERENT
FROM EVERY ONE BUT THE ONE
WHO CAN ADD COLOURS TO MY
LIFE.
WHO CAN PROTECT ME AND SAY
ONE LETS START LIFE FROM THE
BEGNING .FROM THE CHILDHOOD
I LOST IN THE DARKNESS.
I WANT TO SEE LIFE FROM DIFFERENT
PERSPECTIVE WHERE ONLY LOVE
EXIST WHERE ONLY FOREVER
WORD EXIST .
EMOTIONS CANT EVEN BE SEPRATED
FROM THE DEATH .
WHERE NOTHING MATTER EVEN
IF WE LOST TO WHOLE WORLD
WE CAN SMILE AGAIN FOR HAVING

EACH OTHER AND SAY WE CAN
TAKE ANY RISK TO HAVE US .
WHERE TIME CANT CHANGE AND
FADE EMOTIONS .THE EMOTIONS
ARE DEEPER THAN OUR OWN
HAPPINESS .
EVEN WHEN WE TURN TO HUNDRED
THE LOVE WOULD BE LIKE THE
DAY ONE .
MAY BE I AM SEARCHING FOR
SOMETHING WHO CAN LOVE
MY SOUL AND HOW MUCH
FLAWS I HAVE WHO CAN
PROUDLY SAY I AM OK WITH IT .
BEFORE THE PERSON I DON'T NEED
TO HIDE MY BROKEN PIECES AND
EVEN I FALL APART WHO CAN
LEND ME HIS SHOULDER BY
SAYING CRY HOW YOU WANT TO
ITS OK TO BE BROKEN WHO CAN
ACCEPT THE MYSTERICAL ME .
MAY BE SOMEONE WHO CAN SEE
THE BEAUTIFUL AND INNOCENT
SOUL I HAVE .
WHO CAN SEE MY WORTH .
MAY BE THE RELATION WHERE
EVEN WHOLE WORLD LEAVE
OUR HAND WE COULD STAND
BY EACH OTHER CHEERISH EACH
OTHER NOT BOTHERING ABOUT
THE WHOLE WORLD .
WHEN WE BOTH COMPLETE
OUR WORLD .

WHOM WE CAN EACH OTHER AND
CAPABLE OF PLAYING EVERY
RELATIONSHIP IN OUR LIFE.
WHERE ONE PAIN GETS TEARS TO
THE ANOTHER EYE.
WHO CAN SACRIFICE EVERYTHING
TO HOLD HANDS .
WHO CAN WRITE A DIFFERENT
HISTORY OF LOVE .
THE LOVE WHICH ONLY FOUND
IN FAIRYTALES AND BOOKS
WHO CAN MAKE IT TRUE AND
CAN NARRATE HOW BEAUTIFUL
LOVE CAN BE .
THE LOVE WHICH CANT BE ERASED
BY THE AGES .
ADDING A NEW CHAPTER AND
A NEW STORY TO LOVE .
WHERE EXCEPT TIME NOTHING
CAN BE MORE PRECIOUS .
MAY BE LOVE SHOULD BE LIKE
A FAIRY TALE WHICH IS CREATED
BY THE DIFFERENT DESTINY DIFFERENT
TIME BUT SHOWING UP IN THE DREAMS
AND CONNECTING TO THE PERSON
EVEN IN THEIR ABSENCE MAY BE
SOMETHING WHICH ALWAYS
REMAINED UNEXPLAINED
BETWEEN US .
MAY BE I HOPE YOU SHOW UP
BEFORE IT TO LATE AND MAKE ME
TRUE THAT I AM NOT WRONG
MAY BE SOMEWHERE IN THIS

EARTH YOU EXIST .
THIS TIME AND PLACE CANT MAKE
DISTANCE BETWEEEN US .
I FEEL YOU WITHOUT KNOWING
YOUR EXISTENCE MAY BE I DON'T KNOW
WHERE ARE YOU IN THIS WORLD
BUT ONE DAY I WILL FIND YOU FOR
SURE EVEN IF YOU EXIST IN DIFFERENT
WORLD.
THEIR IS SOMETHING IN THIS WORLD
WHICH WE COULDNOT CHANGE OUR
DESTINY AND US BEFORE KNOWING
OUR HEART KNEW EACH OTHER .

MAY BE PEOPLE DON'T UNDERSTAND THIS
CONNECTION PEOPLE CALL CRAZY BUT
EXCEPT US NO ONE KNOWN THE DEPTH
OF OUR EMOTIONS .
MAY BE I DON'T KNOW WHAT
SHOULD I NAME THIS RELATION .
WHAT SHOULD I NAME THIS
CONNECTION BECAUSE I DON'T
KNOW WHAT IS THIS BUT WHEN
ONE DAY I WILL SEE YOU .
I WILL UNDERSTAND THE DEPTH
OF US .
MAY BE OUR RELATION IS BEYOND
HUMAN IMAGINATION .
THIS WAIT DOESN'T HURT MORE
BECAUSE I KNOW ONE DAY YOU

WILL FIND ME AND EVERY
BROKEN PIECE OF ME YOU WILL
FIX IT .
THE DAY YOU WILL KNOW WHY
YOU WAS NOT HAPPY AFTER
HAVING EVERYTHING IN LIFE.
THAT DAY I WILL HOLD YOU AND
TAKE YOU TO THE WORLD OF
HAPPINESS .
WITHOUT KNOWING OUR SOULS
ALREADY CONNECTED LIKE ITS
BEEN WAITING FOR THE AGES .
YOU WILL FIND EVERY ANSWER
FOR YOUR PUZZLES .
MAY BE WITHOUT KNOWING WE
SHARE THE SAME PAIN AND SAME
HAPPINESS .
WHEN HEART FEELS BURDEN SEE
ME MAY BE I WAS BREAKING LIKE
THE SAME WAY WITH THE HIDDEN
SCAR ON MY SOUL AND EXCEPT YOU
NO ONE CAN FEEL THE HIDDEN PAIN
I HAVE .
MAY BE WHEN I FEEL BURDEN I
WILL SAY TO MY HEART THAT WE
ARE NEVER APART I AM THERE WITH
YOU EVEN IN THE DARKNESS OF NIGHT
I WILL ADD COLOURS TO YOUR BROKEN
SOUL .
MAY BE I COULD NOT NAME THIS
RELATION BUT I WILL ALWAYS SAY
YOU TO BELIEVE IN ME .
I WILL FIND YOU ONE DAY .

PLEASE BELIEVE ME EVEN THROUGH
I AM NOT WITH YOU BUT YOUR
SOUL KNOWS ME .
IN MY EYES YOU WILL FIND REASON
FOR YOUR EXISTENCE .
WHEN YOU WILL FIND ME MAY BE
THAT DAY YOU WILL FIND YOUR
HAPPINESS AND UNDERSTAND
WHAT YOUR SEARCHING FOR THE
AGES .
MAY BE THE DAY YOU SEE ME
YOUR WORLD CHANGES
WITHOUT EXPECTING ANYTHING
WILL YOU SEARCH FOR ME ?
CAN YOU RECOGNIZE ME EVEN
IN THE WORLD OF LAKHS ?
CAN YOU FIND ME IN THIS MAZE .
I AM WAITING UNDER THIS DARKNESS
TO FIND ME AND TAKE ME TO THE
ANOTHER WORLD WHERE WE
ALREADY MEET .
THE WORLD WHERE OUR SOULS MEET .
MAY BE THIS STORY HITS DIFFERENT
BECAUSE THIS STRANGE FEELINGS
ONLY EXIST IN MOVIES .
MAY BE THIS LIFE FEELS SO
MYSTERIOUS .
MAY BE THE DAY WE MEET WE
UNDERSTAND THE REASON WHY
WE ARE ALONE ALL THE AGES
MAY BE THAT DAYS WE UNDERSTAND
WHY OUR LIFE HAS NO COLOURS
AFTER HAVING EVERYTHING.

LETS ACCEPT EACH OTHER FLAWS
ACCEPTING THE WAY IT IS .
MAY BE OUR LIFE HAS REFLECTION
OF EACH OTHER .
WE ARE THE MEANING FOR EACH
OTHER .
MAY BE WE ARE THE REAL EXAMPLE
OF TRUE LOVE AND PAST LIFE
CONNECTIONS.
WHERE OUR SOUL UNDERSTAND
EACH OTHER WITHOUT KNOWING
WE ARE .
WE LIVED IN A WORLD WE SPENT
OUR HAPPINESS AND SADNESS
WITH EACH OTHER .
I FIND A HOPE IN YOUR EYES .
I SEE MYSELF IN YOU .
I SEE A BROKEN MIRROR IN YOU.
I HAVE A PART OF YOUR HEART .
WE ARE NOT DIFFERENT WE ARE
THE SAME PERSON WITH DIFFERENT
BODIES YOUR PAIN WILL REACH TO
MY HEART WITHOUT BEING
EXPRESSED FOR ME .
IF I GET A CHANCE I WOULD
HOLD YOU AND GIVE MYSELF
TO YOU AND HEAL YOUR
BROKEN CHILD .
THE CHILD WHO STUCKED IN
DIFFERENT TIME .
I WILL HOLD YOURS HAND
AND PROTECT YOU TO END OF
MY LIFE .

YOU HAVE WAITED FOR THIS
DAY .
MAY BE YOUR THE REASON
FOR MY EXISTENCE THE
REASON I WAS ALONE ALL
AGES WITHOUT KNOWING
WHAT I WANT IN MY LIFE .
CAN WE WRITE A STORY
WHICH IS WRITTEN BY THE
BLEED OF LOVE .
CAN I STAY IN THIS DREAM
FOREVER .
MAY BE THIS IS SOMEWHERE
I CAN HAPPILY HOLD YOUR
HAND .
MAY BE OUR STORY IS SO
COMPLICATED BECAUSE WE
CRAVED FOR THE LOVE OF
EACH OTHER .
WE ARE ALONE EVEN AFTER
HAVING EVERYTHING .
WE STOOD UP BY YOURSELF
EVEN WITHOUT KNOWING
EACH OTHER .
I WANT TO KNOW YOU I WANT
TO SEE YOU .
I AM THE SLAVE OF THIS DESTINY
COULDNOT BE ABLE TO THERE
WHEN YOU CRIED ALONE IN
NIGHTS.
I COULDNOT STAND BY YOURSELF .
I AM SURE OUR STORY WILL BE A
MIRROR MAY BE THE REASON

WE UNDERSTAND THE DEPTH
OF THIS FEELINGS.
DO YOU TRIED TO SEARCH ME?
DO YOU BELIEVED IN YOURSELF
THAT I WOULD STAND BY
YOURSELF NO MATTER HOW
WORSE SITUATIONS ARE .
WE CAN FEEL EACH OTHER .
THE PAIN WE ARE FACING WE
WILL SMILE TOGETHER .
EVEN IF I HAD ONE DAY LEFT
IN MY LIFE .
I HAPPILY LEAVE THIS WORLD
BY SEEING YOU.
MAY BE I DON'T KNOW IF
THAT DAY COMES OR NOT
MAY BE I NEVER SHARE THIS
FEELING BECAUSE NO ONE CAN
UNDESRSTAND THE DEPTH OF
THIS FEELINGS EXCEPT YOU .
WE ARE THE BROKEN MIRROR
WHICH CAN NEVER BE FIXED
WITH OTHERS.

YOU WALKED IN MY DREAM WITH
THE BLURRY FACE OF YOURS .
THE PRESENCE JUST ADDS MEANING
TO MY EXISTENCE .
DON'T ASK ME WHY I WAS LIKE
THIS BUT I JUST BELIEVED THAT

YOU WILL ALSO FIND THE WAY
FOR ME .
I HIDED MYSELF IN THE RAYS
OF MOON .
SEE ME NOW , HEAR ME NOW
IN YOUR HEART AND FOLLOW
THE VOICE OF YOUR DREAMS .
WE WILL FIND OURSELVES
ONE DAY LIKE EVERYTHING
MAY BE OUR HEART KNOWS
THE STORY .
EVEN IN THOUSANDS OF PEOPLE
WE WILL FIND EACH OTHER .
I HOPE THAT DAY COMES FAST.
WHERE I COULD SEE YOU AGAIN .
LIFE GOES ON WITH SO MUCH BURDEN .
EVERYTHING FEELS SO WORRIED .
MAY BE I FEAR IF THIS COULD TURN
TO A DREAM .
I FEAR OF TURNING THIS BEAUTIFUL
FEELINGS INTO DREAM .
I WISH YOU NEVER CHANGE AND
BELIEVE IN THAT FADED DREAM .
I AM SCARED OF GETTING
FORGETEN BY YOU .
MAY BE I FEAR THAT I WILL LOOSE
REASON OF MY LIFE .
I AM SCARED THAT I COULDNOT
IMAGINE MYSELF WITHOUT
THAT DREAM .
THE DREAM TO BE WITH YOU .
THE DREAM TO SEARCH YOU
THE GAME OF LIFE STARTS IN

GROUP OF PEOPLE WE FORGET
TO SEARCH EACH OTHER BY
ADJUSTING WITH ANOTHER OR
TO RELY ON A DREAM AND
SEARCH FOR EACH OTHER .
THERE IS SOMETHING SPECIAL
IN YOU AND ME THERE COULD
BE NO OTHER RELATION WHICH
IS LIKE US SOMETIMES I FEEL IS
THERE ANY CAST SPELLS YOU .
SHOULD I ADD BEAUTIFUL COLOUR
IN MY EVERY WORD BECAUSE IT
DESCRIBES YOUR BEAUTIFUL
EXISTENCE .
SOMETIMES I WISH I COULD HAVE
MAGIC AND SEARCH YOU IN EVERY
HUMAN I SEARCH FOR.
THIS LETTERS ARE JUST NOT
LETTERS THIS IS BEAUTY OF WORDS
TO EXPRESS HOW MEAN YOU ARE
TO ME .
MAY BE I THINK SOMETIMES ARE
YOU IN ANOTHER WORLD ?
WHAT IS YOUR NAME ?
HOW YOU WILL GONNA FIND
ME?
DO YOU REMEMEMBER ME ?
I THOUGHT TO FORGET YOU
AND MOVE ON IN MY LIFE BUT
EVERYTIME I TRY TO RUN AWAY
MY HEART FEELS SO BURDEN.
MAY BE I FEEL CRAZY ABOUT
MYSELF HOW COULD I PROBABLY

MISS SOMEONE WHOM I NEVER
KNOWN WILL CONSTANTLY
THINKING OF YOU WILL CHANGE
ANYTHING ?SOMETIMES I BLAME
MYSELF FOR BEING SENSETIVE OVER
MAY BE THAN I REALISE YOUR BLUR
FACE WHICH COMFORTS ME EVEN
IN MY HARDEST TIME .
I WILL SPEAK WITH YOU ONE DAY .
I CAN FEEL YOU EVEN WITHOUT
KNOWING .
SO REMEMBER TO BE STRONG AND
CARE FOR YOURSELF BECAUSE
YOU'RE A MIRROR TO ME .
YOUR THOUGHTS WILL REFLECT ME.
I WILL NEVER SHARE MY THOUGHTS
I FEEL INSECURE WITH THE FEELINGS
I HAVE ABOUT MY VISIONS .
MAY BE THAN I FEEL HOW YOU
HANDLE THIS ALONE .
MAY BE I WAIT FOR THAT ONE DAY
WHERE I CAN SEE YOU AND ASK
EVERY QUESTION IN MY HEART
STILL GETTING CLEAR OF MYSTERY .
I KNOW SOMEWHERE THAT ONLY
YOU CAN ANSWER THIS .
EVERYTHING IS NOT COINCIDENCE
WE MAY STARTED IT FROM FUN BUT
THIS BECAME AN IMPORTANT ASPECT
IN OUR LIFE .
WE WROTE OUR DESTINY BY OURSELF
AND WITHOUT KNOWING WE BECAME
A SINGLE SOUL.

I STOPPED CHASING FOR YOUR LOVE
AND YOU BECAUSE SOMEWHERE
I UNDERSTAND WE HAVENT CHOOSEN
OURSELF BUT OUR DESTINY CHOOSED
US.
WHEN DESTINY CHOOSED US IT
MIGHT HAVE A CERTAIN PLAN
AND TIME .
I WILL WAIT FOR THAT TIME WHEN
THE DESTINY BRING US TOGETHER .
MAY BE TRUE LOVE IS WORTH
WAITING FOR .
TO GET A TRUE LOVE WE NEED TO PAY
HIGH PRICE TO GET LOVED BUT DON'T
WORRY I WILL STAND IN THE FROZEN
DIM LIGHT WAITING FOR YOU.
IT MIGHT BE DAYS ,MONTHS OR
AGES I WILL STAND BY THEIR TO
FIND ME .
STILL THEN I WAIT IN THIS
FROZEN LIGHT WAITING BY
SEEING MOON .
THE WAY THERE ARE THOUSANDS
OF STARS BUT ONE MOON I WANT
YOU TO FIND MYSELF IN BETWEEN
GROUP OF PEOPLE.
I AM NOT AWARE OF PAST LIFE
COMPLETELY I AM NOT SURE
WHAT HAPPENED BUT I AM SURE
THAT YOU ARE SOMEONE
I AM WAITING FOR THE AGES.
I COULD LOVE YOU THOUSAND
TIMES EVERY DAY .

EVEN IF YOU WEAR A MASK OF
OTHER I COULD FIND YOU.
I CAN FEEL YOU BY NOT KNOWING
WHO YOU ARE .
I WISH WE COULD FIND EACH
OTHER .
WHEN I READ THE PROVERB
OF REAL THREAD I REMEMBER
YOU MAY YOU AND ME HAVING
AN INVISIBLE RED THREAD
WHICH CONNECTS EACH OTHERS
WE MIGHT BE IN DIFFERENT WORLD
BUT ONE DAY WE WILL BE TOGETHER .
THIS IS OUR DESTINY FOR ALL
THE PAIN WE HAVE GONE THROUGH
THE REASON WE COULDNOT BE ABLE TO
ACCEPT ANYONE AND GO THROUGH
ANY RELATION BECAUSE WE ARE
ALREADY ENGAGED IN THE WORLD
OF DIVINE POWER .
BELIEVE ME I WILL SEARCH FOR
YOUR EXISTENCE ME DAY .
STILL THEN BE STRONG .
THIS ARE LETTERS OF MY HEART
WHICH IS ALWAYS UNSAID .
DONT HURT YOURSELF MAY BE
WE COULD MEET IN THE WORLD
OF DIVINE .
STILL THEN UNDERSTAND
EVERY HINT AND LYRICS
EVERYTHING IS NOT COINCIDENCE .
IT IS MEANT FOR US.
I AM STANDING ALONE WITH A HOPE

TO SEE YOU.
CAN WE GO BACK TO TIME AND
WRITE OUR STORY BY OURSELF.
THE REASON YOU COULDNOT
MOVE ON .
I AM WAITING FOR YOU .
EVEN LIFE GIVES HUNDRED OF
CHANCES TO MOVE ON FROM
YOUR THOUGHTS I WILL NEVER YOU .
WILL NEVER LEAVE YOU .
I SHOW MY ALL LOYALITY WAITING
FOR THIS PROCESS EVEN ONE DAY
IT BECOMES HARD TO BREATHE WITH
YOUR BLUR VISIONS.
MAY BE MY SURROUNDING
BECOME BLUR WHEN I STAND
ALONE WITH LACK OF CLEAR .
MAY BE WHEN SOMEONE ASK
WHAT I AM WAITING FOR THEN I
DON'T HAVE AN ANSWER. I DON'T
KNOW HOW TO CONVEY MYSELF.
WILL THIS LIFE BECOME A MOVIE .
IS THIS FEELINGS ARE REAL OR
ILLUSIONS .
I AM NOT AWARE OF BUT I KNOW
WITH YOUR MEMORIES I AM REALLY
HAPPY .
YOU COMPLETE ME .
I HAVE LOST IN THIS WORLD
CAN YOU MAKE ME ALIVE ?
CAN YOU SHOW ME THE COLORS
OF LIFE?
CAN YOU MAKE ME BELIEVE MY

FAITH TOWARDS YOU IS NOT
AN ILLUSION .
YOU ALSO NEVER FORGET ME
AND HIDED YOUR FEELINGS
FOR SO LONG CAN YOU MAKE ME
BELIEVE THAT LOVING YOU
WAS THE BEST THING I EVER DID
IN MY LIFE ?
CAN I FIND MY HAPPINESS
ONCE AGAIN ?
MAY BE EVEN IF I WRITE ALL
PAGES MY FEELINGS STILL
FEEL UNEXPRESSED .
LETS GO TOGETHER THE WORLD
WHERE THE PEOPLE UNDERSTAND
THE MYSTERY .
MAY BE OUR LOVE IS ANOTHER
MYSTERY TO THE WORLD.
SOMETIMES WITHOUT KNOWING
I AM GIVING UP ON YOU .
MAY BE I THINK I SHOULD STOP
HURTING MYSELF TO FIND YOU.
I SHOULD LOVE MYSELF BEFORE
I FIND YOU.
MAY BE I AM SCARE OF THIS DREAM
TO TURNING AS AN ILLUSION .
THE PAIN IN MY HEART IS NOT
HAVING AN END .
MAY BE I FEEL LIKE I AM GIVING
UP ON MYSELF .
MAY BE AT A POINT OF TIME I FEEL
WORTHLESS WITH THIS HONOURS
AND CERTIFICATES .

MAY BE THIS IS NOT I WAITED FOR
SO LONG MAY BE I AM WAITING FOR
SOME MIRACLE TO HAPPEN IN MY
LIFE WHERE I CAN FIND YOU MAY
BE I STAYED STRONG FOR A LONG
TIME ?
IS IT GREEDY TO EXPECT YOU
TO RECOGNIZE ME AND MAKE
ME FEEL HAPPY .
THERE ARE MANY MYSTERY IN
OUR LIFE WHERE ONLY WE CAN
UNDERSTAND MAY BE I AM
COMPLETELY BROKEN I STAYED
STONG FOR A LONG TIME .
I FEEL DISCONNECTED WITH THIS
WORLD MAY BE YOU ARE THE ONLY
ONE WHO CAN UNDERSTAND ME .
I AM A NAGGY PERSON WHO SEND
THOUSANDS OF LINES MESSAGES I
CARE A LOT I EASILY GET HURT WITH
LITTLE THINGS I AM AFRAID OF FACING
YOU.
MY SOUL HAS BROKEN TO MANY PIECES
AND I CANT EVEN FIND THE PIECES
WHICH I HAVE LOST .
CAN YOU HELP ME TO FIND MYSELF
AGAIN .
I DON'T KNOW WHAT SHOULD I NAME
THIS RELATION .
MY SOUL HAS CONVERTED TO THE DARK
SOUL BUT OFTEN BEAUTIFUL THAN
ANYTHING ELSE IN THIS LIFE BECAUSE
IT SAW THE PAIN OF HEART BREAK

WALKED ON THE BLEED OF MY
OWN EMOTIONS BUT STILL SMILED
AND ACCEPTED TO BE DIFFERENT
FROM THE WORLD .
MAY BE NOW I UNDERSTAND LOVE AND
FIRE COMES WITH SAME HAND .
WHEN I HOLDED AN EDGE WITHOUT
KNOWING WE ARE ALREADY BURNING
OURSELVES . WITH THE DEEP THOUGHTS
OF LOVE AND PAIN .
THIS EMOTIONS GONNA BURN US TO
ASHES IF WE TRY TO LEAVE OUR HANDS .
MAY BE WE BOTH ARE WAITING THEN WE
CAN CALL LOVE WHEN IT IS SLIPPED IT
BURN OUR BOTH SOULS.I WALKED AWAY
FROM THE BRIGHTNESS AND EVERY
HUMAN EMOTIONS .
WHEN I FOUND THIS IS BECOMING A
WEAKNESS TO ME .
THE INNER SELF KEEP ON SAYING
I NEED TO STAND ALONE AND WRITE
A DIFFERENT STORY WITH THE
PATH OF DARKNESS .
THE PAIN INSIDE ME STARES TO
THE DEATH .
SOMETIMES THERE ARE THOUSANDS
OF BURNING ASHES INSIDE ME
WHICH IS HIDING OVER ALL
THOSE YEARS .
I CAN FEEL THE DEATH WHEN I
AM ALIVE .
I AM IN SITUATION WHERE
I CANT RUN AWAY OR EITHER

I COULD STAY STRONG .
I CAN CRY THOUSANDS OF TIMES
AND GET UP AND EXPLAIN MYSELF
THAT I AM STRONG BUT THE INNER
ME KNOWS THE DEPTH OF THE PAIN .
MY MIND IS CREATING ILLUSIONS
ITS HIDING OVER ALL TEARS BY
WEARING A MASK OF HAPPINESS .
THE PAIN HAS NEVER ENDING JOURNEY .
I CANNOT CHANGE YOUR PAST YOUR
EXPERIENCE YOUR HARD
TIMES AND PAIN .
I JUST BE THE PERSON WHO ACCEPT
YOU WITH YOUR FLAWS RATHER
THAN EXPECTING FOR THE PERFECTION .
WHEN I SAW YOU IN THE DREAM
WITH THE DIM LIGHT AND
INNOCENT EYES.I FELT LIKE YOU
WAS SAYING I AM THERE FOR YOU
"ARE YOU SURE "
THAT YOU WOULDNOT RUN
AWAY WHEN I AM COLD?
ARE YOU SURE THAT YOU STILL
LOVE ME WHEN I AM A
COMPLETELY MESS ?
WOULD YOU STILL LOVE ME
WHEN I AM BROKEN INTO
PIECES AND HELP ME TO JOIN
EVERY PIECE?
ARE YOU SURE THAT WOULD YOU
AGAIN GIVE ME THE SMILE WHICH
I LOST ?
ARE YOU SURE THAT

YOUR PROMISE WOULD
NOT BE A JOKE.

Printed by Libri Plureos GmbH in Hamburg,
Germany